BILLY'S BUCKET

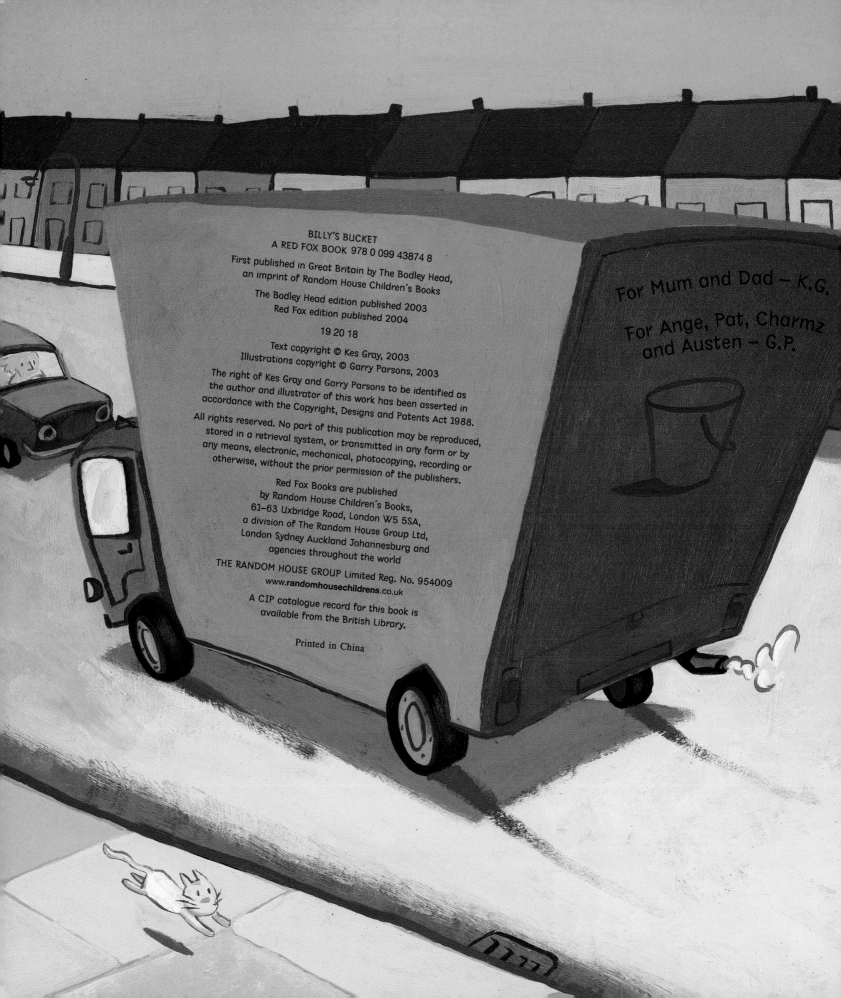

BILLY'S BUCKET
A RED FOX BOOK 978 0 099 43874 8

First published in Great Britain by The Bodley Head,
an imprint of Random House Children's Books

The Bodley Head edition published 2003
Red Fox edition published 2004

19 20 18

Text copyright © Kes Gray, 2003
Illustrations copyright © Garry Parsons, 2003

Red Fox Books are published
by Random House Children's Books,
61–63 Uxbridge Road, London W5 5SA,
a division of The Random House Group Ltd,
London Sydney Auckland Johannesburg and
agencies throughout the world

THE RANDOM HOUSE GROUP Limited Reg. No. 954009
www.randomhousechildrens.co.uk

A CIP catalogue record for this book is
available from the British Library.

Printed in China

For Mum and Dad – K.G.

For Ange, Pat, Charmz
and Austen – G.P.

BILLY'S BUCKET

KES GRAY
GARRY PARSONS

RED FOX

"Can I have a bucket for my birthday?" asked Billy.

Billy's dad looked up from his newspaper.
"**A bucket?** You don't want a bucket for your birthday, nobody has buckets for their birthday."

"Why don't they?" asked Billy.

"Because, Billy," explained his mum, "buckets are . . . well, buckets are far too bucketty to be a birthday present."

But Billy wouldn't be persuaded.
"**Please** can I have a bucket?"
he asked.

"Have a bike,"
said his dad.

"Or some new trainers," said his mum.

"Or a computer game."

"I want a bucket," said Billy. "All right," sighed Billy's dad. "You can have a bucket for your birthday."

"Yippee!" shouted Billy.

The next day,
Billy and his mum and
dad went to Buckets "Я" Us.
There were buckets of buckets at
Buckets "Я" Us: rubber buckets, plastic buckets,
metal buckets, garden buckets, farm buckets,
builders' buckets, seaside buckets and even football buckets.

Billy's mum and dad followed Billy up and down every single aisle.
"What sort of bucket are you looking for?" they asked.
"I don't know," said Billy, "but I'll know it when I see it."

Billy looked long and hard at every single bucket on every single shelf. **"There it is,"** he shouted excitedly, **"that's the one I want,** right up there – 19 shelves up, 78 along from the left!"

Billy's mum and dad got someone to help them.

"They all look the same to me," said the shop assistant.

"No, that one's special," said Billy excitedly.

When Billy got home he ran straight into the
kitchen and filled his bucket with water.

"Of course you can, Billy," smiled his dad.

"Of course you did, Billy," laughed his mum.

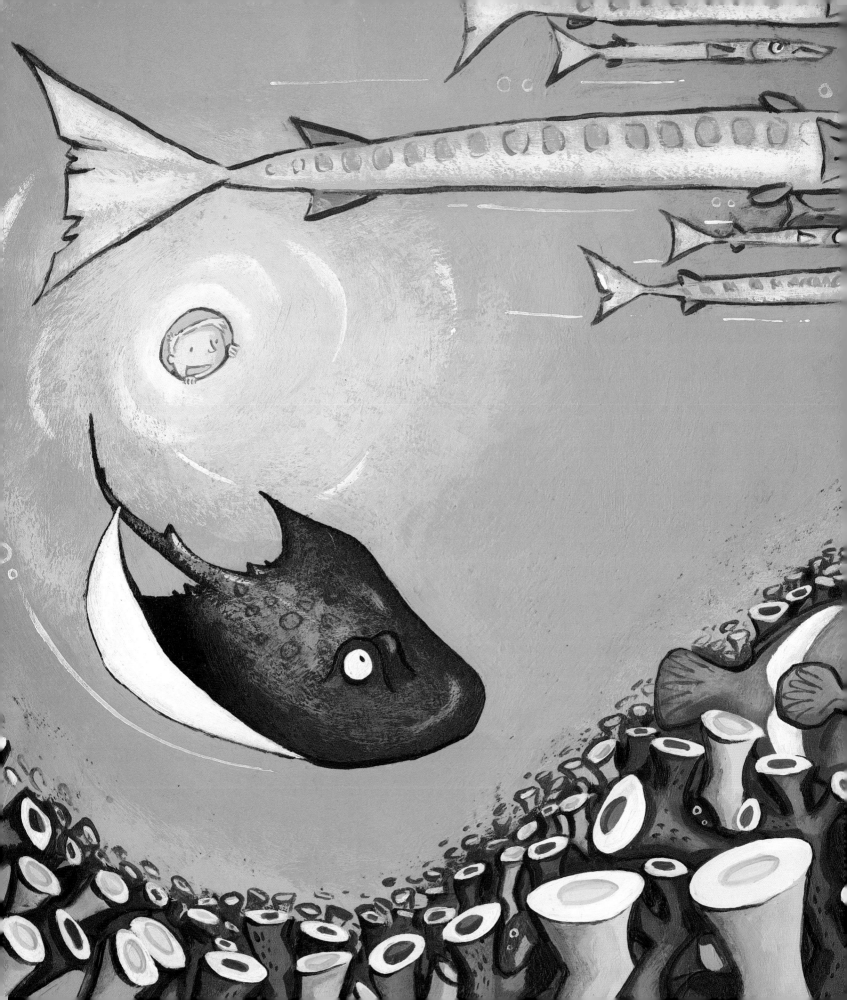

"Guess what I've seen now!" said
Billy, sitting down for his birthday
tea. "I've seen a stingray and some
clown fish and a huge shoal of
barracuda and I think I've seen a
mermaid, but it might have been
a big herring."

"Of course you have, Billy," laughed
his dad.

Billy carried his
bucket to the
lounge.

"What's in your bucket at the moment, Billy?" chuckled his dad.
"Two submarines and a pilchard," said Billy.

"What's in your bucket now, Billy?" giggled his mum.
"Seven sea lions and a walrus," said Billy.
"Of course there are, Billy," laughed his mum and dad.

Billy was still staring into his bucket at bedtime.

Billy's dad nudged his wife and winked. "Billy, is it all right if we borrow your bucket to mix up some wallpaper paste tomorrow?"

Billy looked up from his bucket and frowned. "No it isn't. There are dolphins in my bucket at the moment. You must **never** borrow my bucket."

Billy's mum waited a few moments and winked at her husband. "Billy, is it all right if we borrow your bucket to water the roses with tomorrow?"

Billy looked up from his bucket and shook his head. "There are two scuba divers in my bucket at the moment. You must **never ever** borrow my bucket."

Billy's dad chuckled to himself and waited a few more moments. "Billy, is it all right if I borrow your bucket to clean the car tomorrow?"

Billy looked up from his bucket and sighed. "No, it isn't all right. There's a coral reef in my bucket at the moment.

You must
never
ever
ever
borrow my bucket!"

"What an imagination!" laughed Billy's mum and dad. "Time for bed!"
Billy put his bucket away and went upstairs.

"Thanks for a lovely birthday!" he said.
"And the best present in the world!"

When Billy woke up the next morning he got dressed quickly and ran downstairs to play with his bucket.
But it wasn't there.

"I told you not to borrow my bucket," said Billy.

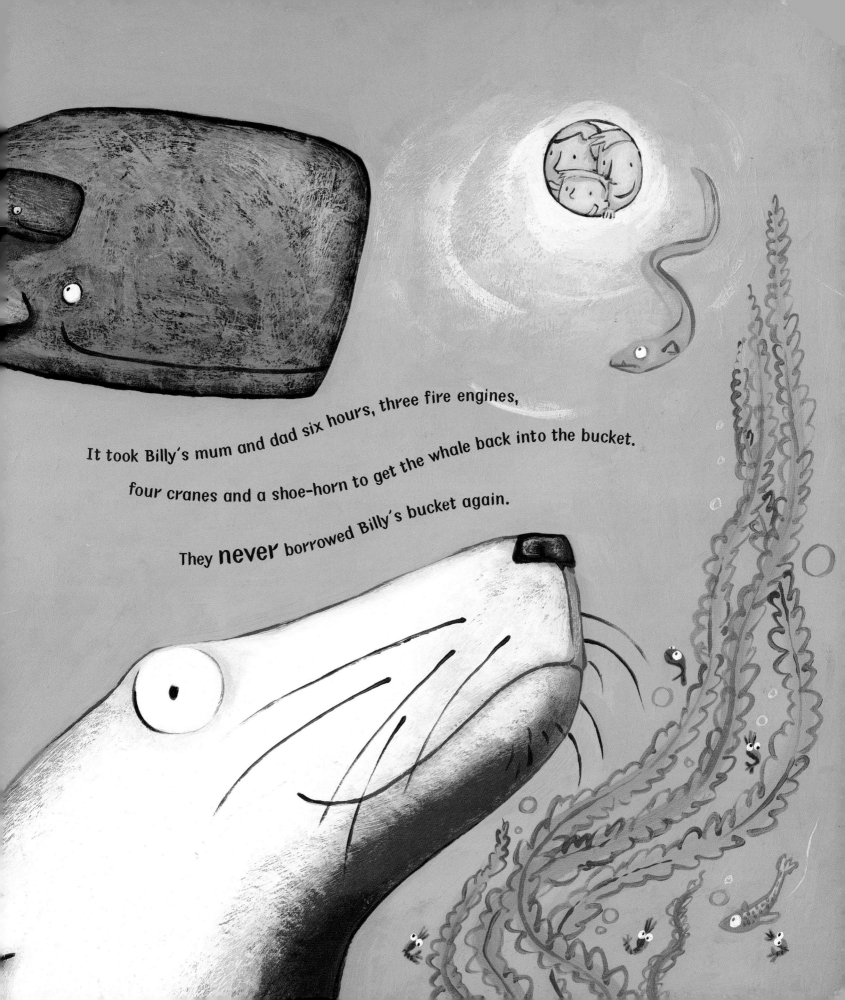

It took Billy's mum and dad six hours, three fire engines,

four cranes and a shoe-horn to get the whale back into the bucket.

They **never** borrowed Billy's bucket again.

If you liked Billy's Bucket — try these . . .

Illustrated by Garry Parsons

Digging for Dinosaurs
by Judy Waite

Written by Kes Gray

Who's Poorly Too?
illustrated by Mary McQuillan

Our Twitchy
illustrated by Mary McQuillan

The Daisy Books:
illustrated by Nick Sharratt

Eat Your Peas

Really, Really

You Do!

Yuk!